Nate the Great
and The
STOLEN BASE

Nate the Great
and The
STOLEN BASE

by Marjorie Weinman Sharmat

illustrations by Marc Simont

A YEARLING BOOK

Published by Yearling, an imprint of Random House Children's Books
a division of Random House, Inc., New York

Visit us on the Web! www.randomhouse.com/kids

Educators and librarians, for a variety of teaching tools,
visit us at www.randomhouse.com/teachers

ISBN-13: 978-0-440-40932-8
ISBN-10: 0-440-40932-2

Reprinted by arrangement with The Putnam Publishing Group Inc.
Printed in the United States of America
One Previous Edition
New Yearling Edition May 2006
45
UPR

For my father, Nathan "Nate" Weinman,
and with appreciation to all the Nathans everywhere
who feel a special bond with Nate the Great

I, Nate the Great, am a detective.
Sometimes I'm a baseball player.
This morning I was a detective
and a baseball player.
My dog, Sludge, and I
went to the field.
I had to practice batting
and running and fielding.
I belong to a team.

ROSAMOND'S RANGERS.

Rosamond, Annie, Harry,

Oliver, Esmeralda, Claude,

Finley, and Pip belong too.

They were at the field.

Rosamond's four cats were there.

They are the team's mascots.

Annie's dog Fang was there.

Fang is not on the team.

He is not a mascot.

Fang should have stayed home.

Rosamond came up to me.

"We can't practice today," she said.

"Somebody stole second base."

"We can get another second base,"

I said. I bent down

and picked up a big stone.

"A stone for second base?"

Rosamond said.

"Not while I'm coach.

Everybody uses stones.

Rosamond's Rangers do not."

Rosamond is a strange coach.

That was no surprise.

Rosamond is a strange person.

She said, "When we play

baseball, I bring first base.

Oliver brings second base.

And Annie brings third base."

Rosamond held up a

large tuna fish can.

"Here's today's first base.

Nobody stole it."

Annie held up a large dog bone.

"Here's today's third base," she said.

"Nobody ate it."

Fang and Sludge sniffed.

Oliver said,

"I was going to bring

the same base I brought yesterday.

But somebody stole it.

It was the best."

I, Nate the Great, did not think

Oliver's second base was the best.

It was an octopus

made of gloopy purple plastic.

Oliver collects eels.

He is saving up

for a real octopus.

"We need a detective to find

my second base," he said.

"Make another octopus," I said.

Oliver was mad.

"You think it's easy to make

those long, curling arms?" he said.

"Besides, that was

my good-luck octopus."

"Very well. I, Nate the Great,

will take the case."

I knew what Oliver's

octopus looked like.

It had eight long, curling arms.

It looked oozy and slimy.

"Where do you keep

your octopus?" I asked.

"On my bookcase," Oliver said.

"But when I went to get it

this morning, it wasn't there."

"We must go to your house," I said.

I wrote a note to my mother.

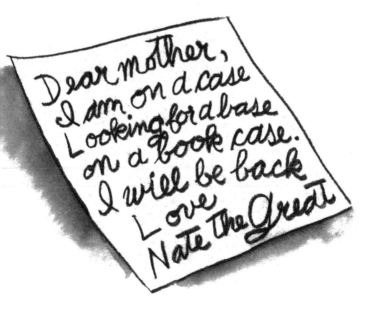

Dear mother,
I am on a case
Looking for a base
on a book case.
I will be back
Love
Nate the Great

I left the note at my house.

Then Sludge, Oliver, and I

went to Oliver's house.

He lives next door.

He took us to his room.

I saw his bookcase.

It was full of books.

So far, so good.

But it was squeezed

in a corner between the wall

and a huge tank of eels.

And the top of it was a mess.

It was covered

with baseball things.

Cards, gloves, balls, and bats.

"I've got so much stuff

on my bookcase

that some of it falls

to the floor,"

Oliver said.

"But I pick it right up."

"This is a real mess," I said.

"Your octopus must
be hidden under something
on top of your bookcase."
I, Nate the Great,
moved things,
piled things,
and sorted things.
Sludge sniffed.

"I have just found
something important," I said.
"What?" Oliver asked.
"A telephone. It was hidden
under two baseball gloves.
And the cord is still hidden."
"The cord goes down the back
of the bookcase

and plugs into the wall,"
Oliver said.

"It's boring.

But the telephone is nice.

I like to call people."

"I know it," I said.

Oliver is a pest.

He follows people.

He calls people.

At last I said,

"I do not see the octopus

on your bookcase."

"So you can't find it either,"

Oliver said.

"*On* is only one place to look,"

I said. "*In* is another."

I looked in Oliver's eel tank.

"Your octopus did not fall

in there," I said.

"Perhaps it fell

down one side

of your bookcase."

"But my bookcase

is squeezed between

the eel tank on one side

and the wall on the other,"
Oliver said.
"I, Nate the Great,
need a flashlight."
Oliver gave me a flashlight.
I flashed the light down

both sides of the bookcase.

"The octopus did not slip through,"
I said.

"So you struck out," Oliver said.

"No. There is one more place
to look. Perhaps your octopus
fell down the *back*
of the bookcase."

"But you can't get
back there,"
Oliver said.

"No problem. I, Nate the Great,
can peer over the top."

I leaned forward.

"Ouch!"

I bumped my head.

"The wall is in the way,"
I said. "I can't see down."
I stretched out flat
on the floor
in front of the bookcase.
"Now what are you doing?"
Oliver asked.
"I am flashing the flashlight
toward the floor at the back
of your bookcase," I said.
I, Nate the Great,
saw something.

I reached for it

and pulled it out.

It was not the octopus.

It was a baseball card.

"So *that's* where my

Babe Ruth card went!"

Oliver said.

"I, Nate the Great, say

that your octopus did not fall

down the back of your bookcase."

I walked around the room.

I looked hard.

"I do not see the octopus
anywhere in this room,"
I said. "When was the last time
you saw it?"

Oliver shrugged. "I'm not sure.
When I got home
from the game yesterday,
I pulled it out
of my pocket
and dumped it on my bookcase
with my other baseball stuff."

"Then what?"

"Then I used my telephone.
I called everybody I know."

"I believe it," I said.

"Then I went out and
followed people
for the rest of the day."

"I believe that too," I said.

"What did you do last night?"

"I slept," Oliver said.

I, Nate the Great,
was getting nowhere.

Oliver said, "This morning
when I went to get my octopus,
I couldn't find it."

"Has anyone else

been in this room?"

I asked.

"Only my eels," Oliver said.

"Then I, Nate the Great,

must go out and

look for clues."

"I will follow you,"

Oliver said.

"Stay by your telephone," I said.

Sludge and I went back

to the baseball field.

"The octopus was second base

in yesterday's game,"

I said to Sludge.

"Perhaps there's a clue here."
I saw Rosamond standing
under a tree with her cats.
"I just tossed my baseball mitt
into the air," she said.
"But it came down
on a branch of this tree
and it's stuck there."
I looked up.
I saw the mitt
on a branch.
"My cats can go up
and shake it down,"
Rosamond said.
"My cats are smart.
If Oliver's octopus

wasn't made of plastic,
they could find it.
An octopus is something
like a tuna fish, isn't it?"
I, Nate the Great,
did not want
to think about that.
I walked over
to where second base
had been.
I kicked the dirt around.
I saw something long
and curling
and oozy and slimy-looking.

It was one arm of Oliver's
octopus.

Oliver's octopus had eight arms.

I had found one.

I had solved one eighth
of this case.

"Look for more octopus arms,"
I said to Sludge.

Sludge and I walked
around the field.

The Sludge ran ahead.

He sniffed.

He stopped.

He brought me another octopus arm.

"Good work, Sludge," I said.

We kept looking.

But we could not find

any more octopus arms.

Sludge and I went home.

We had to think about the case.

I made pancakes for myself.

I gave Sludge a bone.

"We are looking for
a purple plastic octopus
with six arms,"
I said. "Or maybe less.
When Oliver took
the octopus home
from the last game,
he dumped everything
on his bookcase.
He did not notice that

32

two arms were missing.

What else didn't he notice?"

I went to the telephone.

I called Oliver.

He answered right away.

"Who did you follow

before you went home

from yesterday's game?" I asked.

"Annie," he said.

"And your octopus was in

your pocket, right?"

"Right," Oliver said.

"Thank you," I said.

I hung up.

"We must go to Annie's house,"

I said to Sludge.

Annie was sitting in front
with Fang.

"I am looking for
octopus arms," I said.

I looked at Fang.

I did not want to do that.

"Your dog will eat almost anything,"
I said. "Like second base."

"Why would he eat
gloopy purple plastic?" Annie said.
She held up a dog bone.
"This is third base
and Fang didn't eat it.
I'm very proud of him."
Fang wagged his tail.
"But Fang isn't perfect,"
Annie said.
That was no surprise to me,
Nate the Great.
Fang stopped wagging.
Annie said, "When Oliver
followed me after the last game,
Fang followed Oliver.
I think Fang snatched

some of the octopus

from Oliver's pocket."

"Aha!" I said. "So second base

was stolen after all."

"Fang only took

one octopus arm,"

Annie said. "And here it is."

Annie handed a very dirty

octopus arm to me.

"I just found this

in my yard," she said.

"Fang buried it there."

"Did Oliver see the snatch?"

I asked.

"No," Annie said.

"He was too busy following me."

"So Oliver's octopus
is missing three arms
and maybe more,
and Oliver doesn't know it,"
I said.
I said good-bye to Annie.
"This case is as good as solved,"
I said to Sludge.
"All we need to find
are a few more octopus arms."
We went to Oliver's house.
Oliver was talking
on the telephone.

Oliver kept talking.

I knew what I must do:

Get down on the floor.

Reach under the bookcase.

And unplug the telephone

from the wall.

But when I had looked

under there for the octopus,

I did not see the plug

or the cord.

They must have been

too high up.

I had to think of something else.

"HANG UP!" I shouted.

It worked.

Oliver hung up.

I held up the three octopus arms.

"I, Nate the Great, found these.

The case is in good shape.

But your octopus is not."

"I know that," Oliver said.

"When I brought it home,

I saw that I had

a five-armed octopus

instead of one with eight arms."

"Why didn't you tell me?"

I asked.

Oliver smiled.

"What difference does that make

to an octopus?

Five are plenty."

It made a big difference

to me, Nate the Great.
I said, "Then I still have to find
a mostly together octopus."
"Right," Oliver said.
I said, "I, Nate the Great,
have struck out.
But I will be back."
Sludge and I went
to the field.
Rosamond and her cats
were gone.
Her mitt was gone
from the tree.
I sat down on a log.

Sludge sat beside me.

I thought about the case.

I had found a telephone,

a baseball card,

and octopus arms.

None of these mattered.

Or did they?

I looked up at the tree

where Rosamond's mitt

had been stuck.

Hmmm.

I thought about the telephone again.

And the octopus arms.

Those *long, curling* arms.

And I knew where the octopus

had to be!

Sludge and I ran back
to Oliver's house.
Oliver was talking
on the telephone.
I started to pull his bookcase
away from the wall.
Oliver hung up.
"I need to look

behind your bookcase," I said.

I, Nate the Great, pulled harder.

Then I peered behind the bookcase.

I saw the telephone cord

plugged into the wall.

And I saw something else.

Stuck on the cord,

with two of its arms

curled around it,

was a five-armed

purple plastic octopus.

The case was solved!

I reached in to grab the octopus.

R-I-P!

The octopus now had four arms.

But that was plenty.

I held up the octopus.

"You found second base!"

Oliver said. "But how

did you know it was there?"

"Your octopus's arms are long

and curling," I said.

"That makes it easy

for them to catch

onto something.

That was a clue.

But I didn't know it
until I thought
about Rosamond's mitt
that had caught
on a branch.
It fell there
after she tossed it.
It should have landed
on the ground.
When your octopus
fell off the back

of your bookcase,

it should have landed

on the floor.

That's where I looked.

But it never got there.

Because its arms were caught

on the telephone cord."

"Hooray!" Oliver said. "Now we

can have baseball practice.

I will call the team."

Oliver made his calls

while I pushed the bookcase back.

Then Oliver, Sludge, and I

walked to the field.

I, Nate the Great,

went up to bat.

I looked around the field.

I saw first base.

A tuna fish can.

I saw second base.

Oliver's four-armed octopus.

Then I saw third base.

The dog bone was there.

In Fang's teeth.

Fang was third base.

I gripped the bat.

I, Nate the Great, hoped

I would strike out.

～Extra～
Fun Activities!

What's Inside

NATE'S NOTES:
The All-American Game

In 2005, more than 73 million fans went to pro baseball games.

In 2005, about two million American kids played Little League ball.

America is the birthplace of baseball! The first amateur teams formed in the early 1800s. Everyone played by slightly different rules.

Alexander Joy Cartwright invented modern baseball. He wrote down the rules in 1845.

Cincinnati

The Cincinnati Red Stockings became the first pro team in 1869.

Baseball is popular outside America too. The game is especially big in Japan. PURE BORU! (That's Japanese for "Play ball!")

NATE'S NOTES: Great Players

These baseball players are some of the all-time greats. Who is your favorite?

NOLAN RYAN had the longest career in baseball. He played for 27 years.

MICKEY MANTLE hit the longest home run ever. He whacked the ball 634 feet in 1960.

634

TY COBB holds the record for the highest career batting average.

HANK AARON hit 755 home runs during his career. That's more than any other major-league player in history.

LOU GEHRIG hit 23 grand slams. A grand slam is a home-run hit with runners on first, second, and third bases.

KEN GRIFFEY SENIOR and his son KEN GRIFFEY JUNIOR played for the Seattle Mariners at the same time. During one game, they hit back-to-back home runs.

DEION SANDERS played in both baseball's World Series and football's Super Bowl.

NATE'S NOTES: Octopuses

An octopus makes a weird base. Octopuses are also weird animals. Nate found these facts at the library:

An octopus has eight legs. Each one is covered in suction cups. Octopuses have no bones. They have no shells. Their birdlike beaks are their only hard part.

Octopuses are very good at defending themselves.

• They can squirt a cloud of thick black ink at predators.
Now you see them,
now—SQUIRT!—
you don't.

• They are great at changing colors. They can hide by blending into the background. They can turn alarming colors to warn off big hungry fish.

• A few octopus species can pretend to be more dangerous fish. They mimic eels. They act like lionfish. Some octopuses creep along the ocean floor pretending to be coconuts. Nutty!

The smallest octopus is the California octopus. Adults are just an inch long.

The largest? The North Pacific octopus. They can grow to 30 feet long and weigh 100 pounds.

Octopuses are smart! They can open jars.

Some even escape their aquariums to search for snacks. (They like crabs.)

STRANGE BUT TRUE:
Adult female North Pacific octopuses have exactly 2,240 suckers. That's 280 on each arm.

11

How to Make Octopus Pops

These pops will cool you off after an afternoon in the outfield. They look like octopuses.

GET TOGETHER:

- 6 small Dixie cups (3-ounce size)
- 2 cups of fruit juice (Any kind will work. Pink or purple juice makes the pops look more octopus-y.)
- 6 craft sticks
- 48 gummy worms (Again, pink or purple ones are best.)

MAKE YOUR OCTOPUS POPS:

1. Pour $\frac{1}{3}$ cup of juice into each cup. Each one should be about $\frac{3}{4}$ full.
2. Put 8 gummy worms in each cup, lining them up around the edges. These are your octopus's legs.
3. Place the cups in the freezer for a few hours.
4. Place a stick in the center of each cup.
5. Return the cups to the freezer. Leave them there overnight.
6. Peel off the cups.
7. Eat your octopus pops!

Funny Pages

Q: Why did the baseball player go to jail?
A: He tried to steal second base.

Q: Why does it get hot after a baseball game?
A: All the fans leave.

Q: What runs around a baseball field but never scores?
A: A fence.

Q: Why didn't Cinderella make the baseball team?
A: She ran away from the ball.

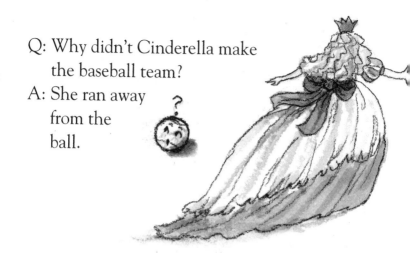

Q: How is a baseball game like a pancake?
A: They both depend on the batter.

Q: What do you call a baseball covered in bugs?
A: A fly ball.

Q: What did the girl octopus say to the boy octopus?

A: I want to hold your hand, hand, hand, hand, hand, hand, hand, hand.

Q: How does an octopus go into battle?

A: Fully armed.

Q: What do you get if you cross a cow and an octopus?
A: A critter that can milk itself.

TV Newscaster: "Eight diamond watches were stolen from a jeweler downtown. Police are looking for a punctual octopus."

Doctor, Doctor, I think I'm an octopus.
I'm sorry, but I can't examine you through this cloud of ink.

30 Teams, 30 Facts

The **Los Angeles Angels** actually play in Anaheim, the home of Disneyland.

Disneyland

President George W. Bush used to own the **Texas Rangers**.

In 1989, the **San Francisco Giants** faced the Oakland A's in the World Series. Play was delayed for 10 days after a strong earthquake hit San Francisco.

The **Dodgers** moved from Brooklyn, New York, to Los Angeles in 1958.

Another team's coach once called the **Oakland Athletics** white elephants. He meant it as an insult. But now a white elephant is the team symbol.

The **Seattle Mariners** play at Safeco Field. The stadium cost $517 million to build. It's the most expensive ballpark in Major League Baseball.

For one game each year, the **Chicago White Sox** let fans bring their dogs to the ballpark.

In 1920, a pitch hit the **Cleveland Indians'** Ray Chapman in the head. He died the next day. Chapman is the only player who has died from a game-related injury. Batting helmets help protect players today.

The **Boston Red Sox** went 86 years between World Series wins. Some fans believed that Babe Ruth, who was traded from the Red Sox to the Yankees in 1920, cursed the team.

The **Kansas City Royals** played their first game in 1969. Just three years later, they finished second in the league.

The **Minnesota Twins** won their first World Series in 1987.

In 2002, the **Detroit Tigers** hosted an octopus-throwing contest.

In 1970, the **Baltimore Orioles** finished 15 games in front of the second-place New York Yankees. The Orioles went on to win the World Series.

The **Tampa Bay Devil Rays** play at Tropicana Field. The field was built to attract a team to Florida. It took eight years before the Devil Rays came.

The **New York Yankees** have won a record 26 World Series.

The **Toronto Blue Jays** are the only major-league team based in Canada.

In 2001, the **Arizona Diamondbacks** won the World Series. The team was only four years old.

The **Colorado Rockies** are famous for their hitting records. One reason? They play in Denver's mountains. The thin air helps the ball travel farther.

No **San Diego Padres** pitcher has ever pitched a no-hitter.

The **Chicago Cubs** haven't won a World Series since 1908.

In 1935, the **Cincinnati Reds** hosted the first major-league night game.

In 1997, the **Milwaukee Brewers** changed leagues. They moved from the American League to the National League.

AstroTurf is named after the **Houston Astros**. The plastic grass was first used in the team's stadium, the Astrodome, in 1966. Real grass wouldn't grow there.

In 1903, the **Pittsburgh Pirates** lost the first World Series ever played. Boston won.

The **Atlanta Braves** won 11 division championships in a row from 1995 to 2005.

In 1993, the **Florida Marlins** finished in sixth place in their league. They finished fifth in 1994. They finished fourth in 1995 and third in 1996. In 1997, they finished second and went on to win the World Series.

Cardinals fans are supposed to be baseball's best. That's why **St. Louis** is nicknamed Baseball City, U.S.A.

LET'S GO METS!

The **New York Mets** were the first team to host an official Banner Day. LET'S GO, METS!

Before 2005, the **Washington Nationals** played in Montreal. They were called the Expos.

In August 1922, the Chicago Cubs beat the **Philadelphia Phillies** 26 to 23. The 49-run score is an all-time game high.

How to Make Caramel Corn

Caramel corn is a great baseball snack. It's nice to eat if you're watching the game on TV.

Ask an adult to help with this recipe.

GET TOGETHER:

- 4 cups of freshly popped corn
- salt
- a shallow roasting pan
- a heavy saucepan
- 1 cup of brown sugar
- $\frac{1}{3}$ cup (1 stick) of butter
- $\frac{1}{2}$ cup of light corn syrup
- $\frac{1}{2}$ teaspoon of vanilla
- $\frac{1}{2}$ teaspoon of baking soda

MAKE YOUR CARAMEL CORN:

1. Preheat the oven to 250 degrees.
2. Lightly salt the popcorn.
3. Place the popcorn in the roasting pan.
4. In the saucepan, mix the sugar, butter, and corn syrup. Get your adult helper to stir the mixture over medium heat until it boils.
5. Boil the mixture for five minutes without stirring.

6. Remove the saucepan from the heat. Stir in the vanilla and baking soda.
7. Pour the mixture over the popcorn. Stir to coat well.
8. Bake for one hour.
9. Cool. Break into small clumps.
10. Eat while cheering on your favorite team!

Have you helped solve all
Nate the Great's mysteries?

❑ **Nate the Great**: Meet Nate, the great detective, and join him as he uses incredible sleuthing skills to solve his first big case.

❑ **Nate the Great Goes Undercover**: Who— or what—is raiding Oliver's trash every night? Nate bravely hides out in his friend's garbage can to catch the smelly crook.

❑ **Nate the Great and the Lost List**: Nate loves pancakes, but who ever heard of cats eating them? Is a strange recipe at the heart of this mystery?

❑ **Nate the Great and the Phony Clue**: Against ferocious cats, hostile adversaries, and a sly phony clue, Nate struggles to prove that he's still the world's greatest detective.

❑ **Nate the Great and the Sticky Case**: Nate is stuck with his stickiest case yet as he hunts for his friend Claude's valuable stegosaurus stamp.

❑ **Nate the Great and the Missing Key**: Nate isn't afraid to look anywhere—even under the nose of his friend's ferocious dog, Fang—to solve the case of the missing key.

❑ **Nate the Great and the Monster Mess**: Nate loves his mother's deliciously spooky Monster Cookies, but the recipe has vanished! This is one case Nate and his growling stomach can't afford to lose.

❑ **Nate the Great, San Francisco Detective**: Nate visits his cousin Olivia Sharp in the big city, but it's no vacation. Can he find a lost joke book in time to save the world?

❑ **Nate the Great and the Big Sniff**: Nate depends on his dog, Sludge, to help him solve all his cases. But Nate is on his own this time, because Sludge has disappeared! Can Nate solve the case and recover his canine buddy?

❑ **Nate the Great on the Owl Express**: Nate boards a train to guard Hoot, his cousin Olivia Sharp's pet owl. Then Hoot vanishes! Can Nate find out *whooo* took the feathered creature?